Tay

By Phelicia Lang

This Book Belongs To

_____

This book is dedicated to my parents
J. B. and Sadie Ross, and my hubby,
Tony. Thank you for telling me I could do
anything I put my mind to.
I believed you. - P.L.

Me on the Page Publishing
https://meonthepage.com/
Copyright © 2019 Phelicia Lang

ISBN-13: 978-1-7338064-0-4

Illustrations Copyright © Phelicia Lang

Book Design by Cassandra Bowen, Uzuri Designs
http://uzuridesignsbooks.com

Tay

By Phelicia Lang

Books
1 & 2

2 EARLY READER
STORIES IN 1!

Illustrated by
Samanta Veliz

Reading Tips

Dear Family,

You are your child's first teacher! Be sure to spend time reading to and with them each day. They also need you to listen to them read. When they are reading, if they get stuck on a word, teach them to use these simple strategies on the next page. Give them some think time before you give them the answer. Soon your little reader will be reading longer and harder books.

Enjoy your child and Happy Reading!

Phelicia Lang

If your child gets stuck on a word...

Look at the picture	👀
Touch each letter and say its sound slowly	bag
Go back and re-read	↩
Skip the word and come back to it	bag and
Go back and read it again	↩

Remember to always think...

- Does my word make sense?
- Does my word look right?
- Does my word sound right?

Tay Goes to Chess Club

This is Tay.

He is very smart.

He likes to spend
time with friends.

Today, Tay will go to chess club.

He puts his board
and pieces in
his bag.

Tay packs his clock.

Tay is ready for
Chess Club!

Tay and his dad walk to the kids club.

They look both ways
for cars.

Tay is at the chess club.

He looks for his
friends.

Tay will wait his turn for the chess master to teach him.

Tay waits patiently.

He walks to the board to learn new moves.

It is time to practice his moves.

He thinks, and thinks of a strategy.

Tay moves his chess piece, and he wins!

He had fun at chess club.

Tay Goes to the Game

This is Tay. He is very smart.

He likes to play sports.

Today, Tay will go
to a game.

He puts on his
jersey.

He puts on his hat
and his shoes.

Tay and his dad are
ready for the game!

They stand in line to
get a ticket.

Next, they stand in line to get food.

Tay always says please, and thank you.

Tay and his dad find their seats.

They cheer for the team.

His team wins!

Tay is happy!

It is time to go home.

Tay had fun at
the game.

About the Author

Phelicia is a loving wife to Tony, mother to four wonderful children and a precious grandson. They have all inspired her journey to find good books to reflect their lives and interests.

As a Reading Specialist she's passionate about finding the right books to help readers connect to stories they love and books that reflect the readers.

Dreaming big dreams and using those dreams and gifts to help others, is the message she shares with her students.

When she's not creating on her computer she can be found Dreaming Big Dreams, reading and shopping.